Shh!

(Don't Tell Mister Wolf)

First published in hardback in Great Britain by Andersen Press Ltd in 1999
First published in Picture Lions in 2000

3 5 7 9 10 8 6 4 2

ISBN: 0 00 664715 4

Picture Lions is an imprint of the Children's Division, part of HarperCollins Publishers Ltd.
Text and illustrations copyright © Colin McNaughton
The author/illustrator asserts the moral right to be identified as the author/illustrator of the work.

The HarperCollins website address is: www.fireandwater.com.
Manufactured in China

Other Preston Pig Stories
Suddenly!

Boo!

Oops!

Goal!

Hmm…

Colin McNaughton

Shh!
(Don't Tell Mister Wolf)

I'm coming to get you!

Collins

An imprint of HarperCollins*Publishers*

Where's Preston?

Is he in the house?

Is he in the shower?

Is he in the garden?

Shh!
(Don't tell
Mister Wolf)

Is he in the street?

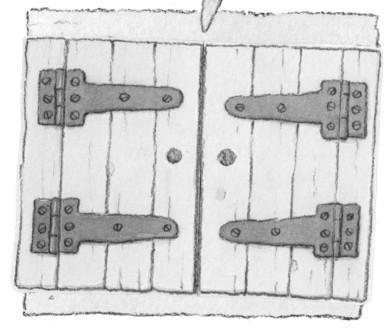

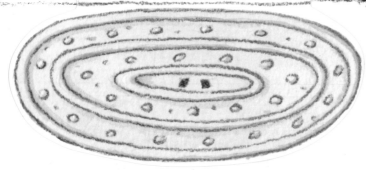

Is he in the park?

Is he in the shop?

Is he in the school?

Is he in the box?

Colin McNaughton was born in Northumberland and had his first book published while he was still at college. He is now one of Britain's most highly acclaimed authors and illustrators of children's books and a winner of many prestigious awards.

Look out for the other fantastic books featuring
Preston Pig and Mister Wolf, of course:

0 00 664654 9   0 00 664520 8   0 00 664522 4   0 00 664521 6   0 00 664655 7

"For sheer fun and verve, Colin McNaughton is unbeatable."
Radio Times

Preston is now starring in his
own television series on